ROSIE'S GLASSES

Dave Whamond

KIDS CAN PRESS

To Mom and Dad, for encouraging me
to do what I love.

All rights reserved. No part of this publication may be reproduced,
stored in a retrieval system or transmitted, in any form or by any
means, without the prior written permission of Kids Can Press Ltd.
or, in case of photocopying or other reprographic copying, a license
from The Canadian Copyright Licensing Agency (Access Copyright).
For an Access Copyright license, visit www.accesscopyright.ca or
call toll free to 1-800-893-5777.

Kids Can Press gratefully acknowledges the financial support of the
Government of Ontario, through the Ontario Media Development
Corporation; the Ontario Arts Council; the Canada Council for the
Arts; and the Government of Canada, through the CBF, for our
publishing activity.

Published in Canada and the U.S. by Kids Can Press Ltd.
25 Dockside Drive, Toronto, ON M5A 0B5

Kids Can Press is a Corus Entertainment Inc. company

www.kidscanpress.com

The artwork in this book was rendered in ink and watercolor.
The text is set in Frutiger Condensed.

Edited by Jennifer Stokes
Designed by Barb Kelly

Printed and bound in Malaysia in 3/2018 by Tien Wah Press (Pte.) Ltd.

CM 18 0 9 8 7 6 5 4 3 2 1

Library and Archives Canada Cataloguing in Publication

Whamond, Dave, author, illustrator
    Rosie's glasses / [written and illustrated by] Dave Whamond.

ISBN 978-1-77138-991-4 (hardcover)

    I. Title.

PS8645.H34R67 2018   jC813'.6   C2017-906775-3